It was Martin Waddell's

perfectly chosen words and

Helen Oxenbury's ever expressive art

which evoked empathy for a little duck the

world over, and made Farmer Duck *an instant*

picture book classic on publication – a book highly

commended for the Kate Greenaway Medal and a

winner of a British Book Award. Now twenty-five

years old, this tale of farmyard friendship and

justice is as powerful and as charming

as ever, and has sold over

two million copies

worldwide.

For Anna
M.W.

For Sebastian,
David & Candlewick
H.O.

First published 1991 by Walker Books Ltd
87 Vauxhall Walk, London SE11 5HJ

This edition published 2016

10 9 8 7 6 5 4 3 2 1

Text © 1991 Martin Waddell
Illustrations © 1991 Helen Oxenbury

The right of Martin Waddell and Helen Oxenbury to be identified
as author and illustrator respectively of this work has been asserted by them
in accordance with the Copyright, Designs and Patents Act 1988

This book has been typeset in Garamond

Printed in China

British Library Cataloguing in Publication Data:
a catalogue record for this book is available from the British Library

ISBN 978-1-4063-6573-3

www.walker.co.uk

FARMER DUCK

written by
MARTIN WADDELL

illustrated by
HELEN OXENBURY

WALKER BOOKS
AND SUBSIDIARIES
LONDON · BOSTON · SYDNEY · AUCKLAND

There once was a duck
who had the bad luck to live
with a lazy old farmer.
The duck did the work.
The farmer stayed
all day in bed.

The duck fetched the cow from the field.

"How goes the work?" called the farmer.

The duck answered,

"Quack!"

The duck brought the sheep from the hill.

"How goes the work?" called the farmer.

The duck answered,

"Quack!"

The duck put the hens in their house.

"How goes the work?"

called the farmer.

The duck answered,

"Quack!"

The farmer got fat through staying in bed
and the poor duck got fed up
with working all day.

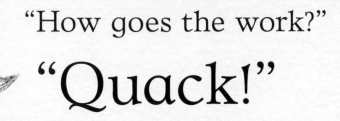

"How goes the work?"

"Quack!"

"How goes the work?"

"Quack!"

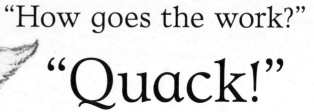

"How goes the work?"

"Quack!"

"How goes the work?"

"Quack!"

"How goes the work?"

"Quack!"

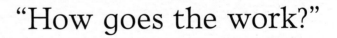

"How goes the work?"

"Quack!"

The poor duck was sleepy
and weepy
and tired.

The hens and the cow and the

sheep got very upset.

They loved the duck.

So they held a meeting under

the moon and they made

a plan for the morning.

"Moo!"

said the cow.

"Baa!"

said the sheep.

"Cluck!"

said the hens.

And *that* was the plan!

It was just before dawn and the farmyard was still.

Through the back door and into the house

crept the cow and the sheep

and the hens.

They stole
down the hall.
They creaked
up the stairs.

They squeezed under the bed of
the farmer and wriggled about.
The bed started to rock
and the farmer woke up,
and he called,
"How goes the work?"
and . . .

"Moo!"

"Baa!"

"Cluck!"

They lifted his bed
and he started to shout,
and they banged and they bounced
the old farmer about and about and about,
right out of the bed . . .

and he fled with the cow and the sheep and the hens

mooing and baaing and clucking around him.

Down the lane . . .

"Moo!"

through the fields . . .

"Baa!"

over the hill . . .

"Cluck!"

and he never came back.

The duck awoke and
waddled wearily into the
yard expecting to hear,
"How goes the work?"
But nobody spoke!

Then the cow and the sheep
and the hens came back.

"Quack?" asked the duck.

"Moo!" said the cow.

"Baa!" said the sheep.

"Cluck!" said the hens.

Which told the duck
the whole
story.

Then mooing and baaing
and clucking and quacking
they all set to work
on their farm.

Martin Waddell is widely regarded as one of the greatest living writers of books for children, and has over 220 published titles to his name. The author of many favourite picture books including *Owl Babies* and the Little Bear series, he has won countless awards for his work, including the prestigious Hans Christian Andersen Medal in 2004. He lives in Newcastle.

Helen Oxenbury is among the most popular and critically-acclaimed illustrators of all time. Her many award-winning books for children include *We're Going On a Bear Hunt*, written by Michael Rosen, and *There's Going to Be a Baby*, written by John Burningham, as well as her classic board books for babies. Helen won the 1999 Kate Greenaway Medal for *Alice in Wonderland*. She lives in London.